The Smallest Whale

Elisabeth Beresford

 Illustrated by
Susan Field

  ORCHARD BOOKS

To the children of Alderney
E.B.

For my husband
S.F.

ORCHARD BOOKS
96 Leonard Street, London EC2A 4RH
Orchard Books Australia
14 Mars Road, Lane Cove, NSW 2066
First published in Great Britain in 1996
First published in paperback 1997
Text © Elisabeth Beresford 1996
Illustrations © Susan Field 1996
The right of Elisabeth Beresford to be identified as author and of Susan Field
as illustrator of this work has been asserted by them in accordance
with the Copyright, Designs and Patents Act, 1988.
A CIP catalogue record for this book is available
from the British Library.
ISBN 1 86039 467 1 (paperback)
ISBN 1 86039 063 3 (hardback)
Printed in Belgium
5 7 9 10 8 6

One sunny day a family of whales were swimming
along in the deep blue sea. Right at the end came
the Smallest Whale. He wasn't supposed to be at the
end. He should have been in the middle near his mother,
but he kept turning to left and right and diving down deep.

The Smallest Whale's mother had the rest of her family to look after and keep in line. She did this by singing to them on a very high note. The sound went up and down, up and down.

"WHEEEWHAAAWHEEEWHAAA..." she went, which means 'follow me'.

But soon the Smallest Whale had fallen so far behind the other whales that he was now closer to a fishing boat than he was to his mother.

"WHEEEWHAAAWHEEEWHAAA," heard the Smallest Whale and he turned and began to follow the fishing boat. It was much the same size as his mother and it was making very nearly the same calling cry. The boat came chugging into the harbour and the Smallest Whale went with it.

Josh leaned over the back of the boat. "Dad, Dad!" he shouted. "There's an enormous whale following us!"

"Watch out!" shouted his father. "It's going to overturn us!" He turned the boat and the Smallest Whale - who did look enormous to Josh - went swimming past.

The Smallest Whale was going so fast he couldn't stop himself and the next moment he had swum right on to the pebble beach. Scrunch!

The poor little whale didn't know what had happened. He just lay there with his sides heaving. He was very, very frightened. There was no familiar call from his mother and there was no comforting water around him.

"Come on, Dad!" said Josh. "We've got to help him."

"We'd only hurt him if we tried to move him," said his father. "But he'll dry out and die if we leave him till the next high tide."

"Then we'll have to keep him wet," said Josh.

"Perhaps the fire brigade could help?" said his father.

"I'll go and tell them," said Josh. "And I'll get all my friends." Then he leant close to the Smallest Whale. "Don't worry, we'll help you."

The Smallest Whale could just hear Josh's voice and his sides heaved even more as he tried to make a sound himself. But no sound came out. There was nothing he could do but lie there and flip his tail in the water as the sea rippled away from him.

"Emergency! Stranded whale on the beach..." shouted Josh and he ran up the high street as fast as he could.

"Emergency! Emergency!" he shouted again as he dashed into the playground. "There's an enormous whale on the beach. Everyone get a bucket or a can and get down there. We've got to keep him wet or he'll die. Hurry. Hurry. Hurry."

Meanwhile, back on the beach the Smallest Whale was gasping and making little clicking noises for his mother. And out in the sea his mother and the family of whales were swimming backwards and forwards calling for him.

"WHEEEWHAAAWHEEEWHAAA!"

But the sound would only travel through water and the Smallest Whale couldn't hear them.

The Smallest Whale didn't hear the fire engine arrive with all the crew. Nor did he hear Josh close behind, running up with all his friends and all the people in the village.

The firemen rattled down the beach and into the water with the hosepipe. And everyone else from the village made a line into the sea and got ready with their buckets and bowls. And when everyone was ready Josh shouted, "One, two, three..."

WHOOSH! The Smallest Whale felt a wonderful splash of cold water on his body. And then another. And another. With every splash he felt better, but he was still too weak to open his eyes.

Whoosh! Whoosh! And again, Whoosh! It was
very hard work for the rescuers. Josh's father stopped
to wipe his forehead. "I don't know whether he's
going to last until the tide comes in again," he said.

"He's not going to dry out!" shouted Josh. "He's not.
He's not! We're going to save the whale."

"Save the whale!" cried all the children and they went to work even faster than before. Whoosh! Whoosh! And again, whoosh!

Very fuzzily the Smallest Whale heard the children's high voices all around him. Their shouting almost sounded like "WHEEEWHAAAWHEEEWHAAA..."

That couldn't, could it, be his mother? And as a little ripple of water touched his tail, the Smallest Whale flicked it feebly.

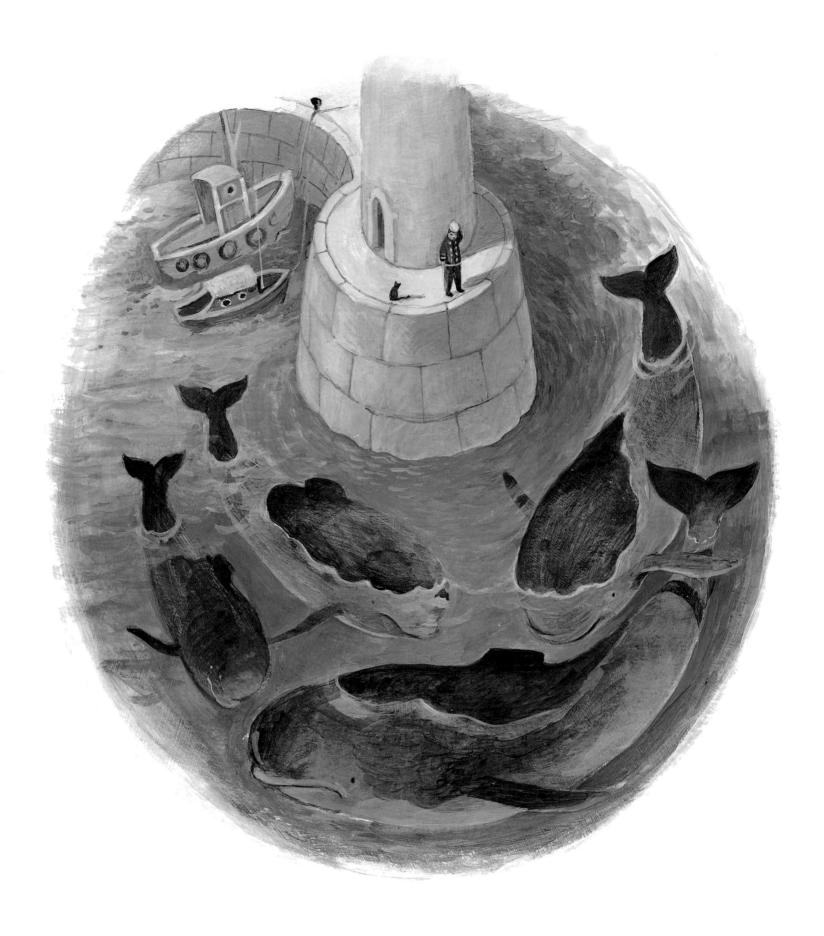

And the Smallest Whale's mother was not so very far away. "WHEEEWHAAAWHEEEWHAAA!" she sang, with all the other whales, as they swam backwards and forwards outside the harbour wall.

Back on the beach the Smallest Whale lay very still.
But the tide was coming in and with each ripple of water
he felt a little better and his tail twitched again.

"We'd better give him a helping hand with the boat,"
said Josh's father.

"WHEEEWHAAAWHEEEWHAAA!..."
The engine started up and slowly Josh's father
turned the boat round and backed towards the beach.

Josh and the children went on pouring water on to
the whale's shiny black back. Whoosh! Whoosh!
And again Whoosh!

The tide was coming in faster now. The firemen
began to wind a thick rope around the Smallest Whale.
And a big wave rolled in, whoosh!

This time it was the Smallest Whale whooshing
as the sea rocked him.

Josh's father quickly fastened the rope to the boat
and then lifted Josh on board.

SPLASH! Another big wave came rolling in. The Smallest
Whale floated for a few seconds. He felt wonderful!
His own weight had been crushing his body. Then the next
big wave came rolling in and it lifted the Smallest Whale
clean off the pebbles.

"One, two, three," called Josh's father. And everyone on the beach pushed with all their strength as the engine of the fishing boat sputtered and whirred.

Suddenly the Smallest Whale was
on the move. Everyone on the beach cheered
and jumped up and down. The Smallest Whale
managed to open his eyes and he made a very small
"WHEEEWHAAAWHEEEWHAAA!" sound. And out at
sea all his family called back to him.
"WHEEEWHAAAWHEEEWHAAA..." Yes, *that* was the
sound he really knew! Not the wheezy old sound of the
fishing boat engine. Suddenly he put his head down
under the waves and dived as hard as he could.

"Whoa!" shouted Josh's father and just in time
he managed to slip the rope.

Splash, crash, wallop.

The Smallest Whale dived down, down, deep
down into the familiar cool sea. And he swam
fast, faster than he had ever swum in his life
before, towards his mother.

"WHEEEWHAAAWHEEEWHAAA," he called to her.

"WHEEEWHAAAWHEEEWHAAA," she sang to him.

Back on the beach the villagers watched the Smallest Whale, far out to sea now, flick his tail and join the rest of his family.

And if Josh and his friends and the people of the village had listened very carefully they might just have heard the Smallest Whale singing to them, "Thank you for saving my life."

"WHEEEWHAAAWHEEEWHAAA..."